EARNEST LEE

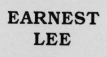

KWI-KWI (KWEE-KWEE)

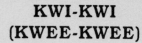

NIGHT-WORM

SKUNKY-STINK SWAMP FISH

THE CASTLE

A MANDERILL

A PEA-POP

GROWL-SLAVVER

EARNEST LEE
AND THE
EMOTION COMMOTION
POLLUTION MACHINE

Written by
Alan Warble

Illustrated by
Manette Wiederhold

ISBN 0-9638527-0-1

Chapter 1

A NEW FRIEND, AN ADVENTURE AND THREE-EYED FISH

The Lees were wee little Pea-Pops.
EVOL, their planet, was polluted purple.
They liked to grumble and gripe.
They liked to fume and fight.
Little Earnest was born a sight.
His face was just not right!
Why Earnest Lee looked so odd was a mystery.
He might just go down in his-story...

"He sure is the ugliest thing I've ever seen," grumbled Drakus.

"Oh, I don't know; I think he's kind of cute," said Sidrene.

Drakus and Sidrene were the older brother and sister of the new baby named Earnest Lee. The newest addition to the Fami-Lee was causing quite a stir in the dirty little hamlet of Grungemudden.

People everywhere soon heard about the ugliest child this side of the Dark Castle. Of course, news always travels fast on the planet EVOL. Especially bad news.

The Pea-Pops were always grousing and complaining, fighting and paining, yelling and straining. Nothing good ever happened on EVOL, and now here was the ugliest baby ever born.

Even his face was different.

Sure, he had one eye like all the other Pea-Pops, but his nose and mouth were both upside down. His nose looked like a heart, and his mouth was always upturned in a smile.

None of the other Pea-Pops ever smiled! Why would anyone want to smile? Their homes were full of garbage. Their streets were strewn with trash. They lived in a world that was forever sullen and colored a dark gray ash.

Why should they clean up their yard when the trash from their next-door-neighbor Pop would just blow in again? It was no wonder that all the adult Pea-Pops were always bickering and all the children were always fighting.

All except one that is: little laughing and smiling Earnest Lee. His laughter rang like music across the wasteland of garbage.

With all the pollution, you wouldn't think there would be much to be happy about. All the Pea-Pops agreed (when they stopped fighting long enough to talk) that the planet EVOL was an awful place to live.

The problem they yelped, as they turned smudged faces toward the north, all came from the Dark Castle. But they only had a small amount of time to shake their fists in anger at the forboding towers that stood out from EVOL's highest mountain before they had to dart for cover.

Acid rains were coming, and the Pea-Pops would get burned if they were caught without protection! EVOL was not only dirty and polluted, but it was dangerous, too.

Ugly dark clouds of red, green, and purple smoke emerged from upper windows of the Dark Castle in endless belches. Murky and vile smelling waters flowed from dark caverns at its base. The polluted liquids flowed in sizzling streams down the sides of the mountain until they came to rest in Skunky-stink Swamp.

"There are terrible monsters that hide in Skunky-stink Swamp!" said Drakus to his buddy, Glombo.

"What do you know, you big lug?" yelled Glombo. "You haven't even taken a step into Forbidden Forest, much less gotten close to Skunky-stink Swamp, you fraidie Pop!"

In a flash, the two Pea-Pops were fighting again; pulling hair, biting and yelling. Of course, that was what they did most of the time.

Fighting was the main occupation of all the Pea-Pops on EVOL.

"What are you guys doing?" asked little Earnest Lee. He wore a red paisley bandanna over his nose and mouth. Earnest Lee looked like some of the TV stars that the Pea-Pop kids watched on Saturday mornings. They were the BAD guys. Of course, EVOL's bad guys were the HEROES.

But Earnest Lee was no hero. His mother had him wear the bandanna to hide his misshapen features. But it really didn't help. The other kids either stole his bandanna and teased him, or they ran and hid from him.

Drakes and Glombo stopped fighting long enough to taunt Earnest Lee.

"Ugly face, has no place, doesn't belong in the Pea-Pop race!" they both sang. Then they started throwing trash at him.

Earnest Lee was such a happy child that he thought they were playing a game with him, and he laughed and tried to jump out of the way. He wasn't as fast as the older boys, and he soon was crying big crocodile tears after they hit him several times.

The older boys grabbed his bandanna and went running off, leaving little Earnest Lee alone, crying. He was used to being alone, and he actually made the best of it by inventing many different games that he could happily play all by himself.

At times he would make a game of seeing how fast he could turn his body from one color to another. All Pea-Pops can change their body colors at will.

Earnest Lee mostly liked to be blue. Sometimes he preferred purple. In his game, though, he changed through all the colors of the rainbow.

Of course he had never seen a real rainbow. It takes a sun to make rainbows, and there was no sun on EVOL. The pollution clouds blotted out the sun forever.

Anyway, it was much too dangerous to look for rainbows when acid rain was falling.

Today Earnest Lee became fascinated by all the tiny creatures on the ground. In fact, he was so distracted watching a column of ants carrying ant-eggs and bits of food that he didn't see the gathering dark rain clouds. The first splash called his attention back to the harsh reality of life on EVOL.

"Ouch!" he said as the droplet of acid rain burned his little arm. He quickly looked around and realized that the closest shelter was under some of the huge gnarled trees on the edge of the Forbidden Forest. Yet, he had been warned by his parents to never go there!

It was rumored that Pea-Pops were never seen again once they entered the dark and treacherous-looking Forest.

Earnest Lee didn't have much choice. It was either seek shelter under the trees' great limbs, or be burned by the terrible acid rain.

Earnest Lee ran as fast as his little legs would carry him towards their protective branches. He dove into the first tree hollow he found, just before the deadly rains started falling.

It was a crashing deluge of rain, and poor little Earnest Lee cringed as he heard the ground sizzle and the mighty trees groan.

Then the thunder and lightning began, and he cowered back even farther into the protective cavity of the great tree. Just when the storm had reached its height, Earnest Lee felt a hand touch his shoulder. He jumped with fright and bumped his head so hard that everything went black.

When he awoke, Earnest Lee was lying in a small underground chamber on a mat made of twined pieces of root. He could see several figures in the shadows barely visible in the dim glow of some night-worms that hung from the ceiling. "Wh-wh-who are you?" Earnest Lee asked in a shaky voice.

"We are called Manderill, and we live in the caverns beneath the forest," said one of the largest of the creatures as it stepped into the light.

Earnest Lee giggled as he looked at the Manderill who now crowded around him. They were even smaller than the Pea-Pops, and were covered with soft orange fur from head to toe. They had little ringed tails, and owl-like faces with two (IMAGINE...TWO!) large quick eyes.

Earnest Lee had never seen anything like them!

One of the larger Manderill, who seemed to be in charge, shooed the rest of the little furry creatures out of the cavern.

"Get some rest, little friend," it said. "You have had a hard bump." Earnest Lee soon dozed off into a nice nap, until he awakened with a start! He felt two big eyes staring at him.

"Whatcha doin'?" asked the wide-eyed little Manderill. "My name is Kwi-Kwi, and I'm not supposed to be here. But I sneaked back anyway."

"You sure do look funny. What kind of critter are you, anyway? Will you be my friend?" the little Manderill blurted out.

Earnest Lee yawned and then laughed.

"You sure do talk a lot," he said. "Of course I'll be your friend."

So Kwi-Kwi took Earnest Lee by the hand and led him into the many tunnels that criss-crossed everywhere. Kwi-Kwi ducked from one passage to another, talking a mile a minute.

"We Manderill are in charge of tending the great trees of the Forest. We keep the roots fertilized, and we protect them from bugs and pests," said Kwi-Kwi. "The trees pay us back by sheltering us from all the pollution outside. All the other Manderill like to live down here tending these stupid old roots, but I don't!"

"I want to be a great explorer and see the world and do all kinds of great deeds. All the others just laugh at me and tell me to get back to digging. I hate these old tunnels, and I want to go outside! I want to breathe outside air and see the sun and stars more than anything else in the world!"

"What are the sun and stars?" asked Earnest Lee. EVOL had been polluted for so long that the Pea-Pops had long forgotten about the sun and stars. Earnest Lee had never even heard about them in nursery-pop school.

"We have stories every sleep-time, and one of the stories is about the Manderill of the past. They lived above ground and frolicked under the hot glowing ball called the sun that brought light and warmth to the world. They laughed with delight at the beauty of a Crystal Castle, and they used to curl up for sleep under a million-bazillion twinkling lights called stars," said Kwi-Kwi. "We also have a tale that one day a hero will come and free the Manderill from our lives of toil beneath the ground. There will be beautiful flowers, and they will be our sign that it is safe to come outside again. I like this story the best of all! The old people tell me that I should be happy here like the rest of them, but I'm not! I hate these old tunnels!"

Kwi-Kwi became so excited that she was running in little circles.

"Would you take me outside, Earnest Lee? Would you take me up to see your world? We could go on an adventure!" Kwi-Kwi said as she quickly skipped and scampered in circles around Earnest Lee.

"Slow down, Kwi-Kwi! You're making me dizzy! Don't you know that EVOL is a polluted and dangerous place?" asked Earnest Lee.

"Please. Pleeeeeeeeeaaaaaasssssssseee, Earnest Lee!!!!!" squeaked Kwi-Kwi in her highest and most plaintive voice.

"Oh, why not. I feel like you're my BEST friend already," said Earnest Lee. "Let's go on an adventure!"

So the two friends set off hand in hand, through the dark and damp tunnels. First they went to the store room where Kwi-Kwi made a pack.

"We might need some rope, and here's a hatchet. That will come in handy," said Kwi-Kwi as she busily darted amongst the shelves filling Earnest Lee's arms with supplies. "And over here's some bread and some mushrooms. And we should also get a blanket."

Kwi-Kwi quickly assembled the supplies into a tidy little backpack. It was almost like she had been planning to leave for a long time.

Finally, the two young explorers were on their way, and they soon emerged from the darkness of the tunnels into the light of the world. Even though the pollution made the light quite dim, it still seemed unbearably bright to the two young friends. Kwi-Kwi even scampered back inside the sheltering dimness of the entrance.

"Do you want to change your mind, Kwi-Kwi?" asked Earnest Lee. Of course, he could understand some of what Kwi-Kwi was feeling because the outside world also made him feel exposed and vulnerable after spending time in the protective confines of the Manderill tunnels.

"N-n-n-no," she stammered, "I don't want to turn back. I want to go see the Crystal Castle. Will you take me there, Earnest Lee?" asked Kwi-Kwi as she slowly crept back into the open.

"Crystal Castle? What Crystal Castle?" Earnest Lee asked. "The only thing that we have here is the DARK CASTLE."

"Then let's go there, Earnest Lee!" exclaimed Kwi-Kwi.

"We can't go there," said Earnest Lee. "All kinds of pollution comes from there! It's probably the scariest place on EVOL!"

"We could make it if we went together," said Kwi-Kwi. "If it's on a high mountain, then we might be able to spot the Crystal Castle from there. Please Earnest Lee, I know we could do it!"

"OK, OK, the Dark Castle it is then!" chuckled Earnest Lee.

So the two friends set off through the Forbidden Forest toward the Dark Castle. The trees of the Forbidden Forest were all twisted and gnarled into frightening shapes by acid rains and the lack of sun. Earnest Lee and Kwi-Kwi were constantly looking over their shoulders or jumping as one of the trees would creak or groan with the wind.

"It sure is scary in here, Earnest Lee," chattered Kwi-Kwi as she urged Earnest Lee along. "Can't you walk any faster?"

"Let's tell stories," said Earnest Lee. "Why don't you tell me some of those stories that you heard in the tunnels, Kwi-Kwi?"

So the two friends began telling each other tales from their childhoods, and they soon forgot their fright. They even began to laugh and sing, and, somehow, this laughter made the whole forest seem a little brighter and a little less scary. All too quickly, they came to the edge of the Forest and the beginning of Skunky-stink Swamp.

"Whew! This sure does stink!" yelped Kwi-Kwi. She still had a good nose for smells because she had lived underground for so long.

Earnest Lee's big eye immediately began to fill with tears and get puffy from all the fumes rising from the foul waters.

"What do we do now, Kwi-Kwi? This swamp is too dangerous to swim across, and besides, I heard my brother say that there are monsters who live in here," fretted Earnest Lee.

"I think we should build a raft," said Kwi-Kwi matter-of-factly. She pulled the small hatchet from the pack, and the two friends collected a large pile of dry wood. They were very careful to not cut any of the live trees. Kwi-Kwi then took a length of rope, and quickly wove it in and out of the timbers with her clever little hands. And before Earnest Lee could blink twice, he was looking at a sturdy raft.

With the raft, Earnest Lee and Kwi-Kwi easily crossed Skunky-stink Swamp. They never did see any monsters, although they did see a large number of three-eyed fish. Earnest Lee even fed them some of the bread from his lunch, and he laughed and laughed when he figured out that he, Kwi-Kwi and the fish all had a different number of eyes.

"I've got one, you've got two, and the fish have three!" he said as he laughed and pointed from his reflection in the water, to Kwi-Kwi, to the fish.

"Do you know what, Kwi-Kwi? We are all different, but none of us is a monster," said Earnest Lee as he watched the swimming fish.

"I thought you were a monster when I first saw you, Earnest Lee," exclaimed Kwi-Kwi. This made them both begin to giggle and laugh again. They were happy until they heard the thunder of the Dark Castle.

CHAPTER 2

THE CASTLE, MACHINE, WIZARDS AND STARS

The two friends reached the edge of the swamp and began their climb up toward the Dark Castle. It looked even more scary now that they were closer, and several times they had to hide from rocks that tumbled down the mountain as the Dark Castle rumbled and shook..

Once little Kwi-Kwi was almost overcome by a large belch of foul smoke that drifted near them. One second, she was talking a mile a minute, and the next second Earnest Lee was frantically fanning his hands in front of her face until she could breathe again.

Finally, they arrived at the gates of the Dark Castle. It was surrounded by a large moat of foul and boiling waters and the drawbridge was closed.

"What do we do now, Earnest Lee?" asked Kwi-Kwi.

This time it was Earnest Lee's turn to come up with a solution.

"Let's sit down and think about it. Then we can make a plan for how we can get into the Castle. We've made it this far, and we can figure this out, too!" he said as he looked at the foreboding Towers.

Kwi-Kwi's plans seemed to have ended with building the raft, and she immediately started cracking jokes and telling funny stories. Earnest Lee was trying hard to concentrate on the problem, but he had a hard time ignoring his friend. Besides, their jokes and laughter helped keep his mind off the roaring noises and all the ugly air and water pollution that was pouring from the Castle.

As they laughed at each new joke, Earnest Lee began to notice a curious thing. Every time they laughed, less smoke issued from the Castle, and the water seemed to get a little cleaner. But he didn't have time to think about this for long...

"WHAT ARE YOU DOING HERE!?" said a tremendous voice that frightened the two friends so much that they each tried to crawl under the other. Kwi-Kwi was quicker and little Earnest Lee was left to deal with the huge intruder.

"We-we came to see the Castle," he managed to squeak out.

"CAN'T YOU SEE IT FROM WHERE YOU LIVE?" rumbled the guardian of the Castle. He was a large, hairy beast with huge dark feet, a great shaggy mane, a long tail that twitched from side to side, and two fangs that poked from his whiskered snout. The only thing that seemed out of place were his large friendly hands.

Earnest Lee thought carefully as he considered his next answer.

"Begging your pardon sir, what I really meant is that we came to pay a visit," he said as he put on his best smile.

Well why didn't you say so?" said the weathered old creature. "I haven't had any visitors in more than 400 years."

"Please sir," said Earnest Lee, "what kind of being are you?"

"I am a Grundlebork. Growl-slavver by name; like my father, and his father, too. I take care of the Eee Cee Pee Machine in the Castle. Our kind was chosen to care for the Machine way back in the distant past when there was still a sun and when the wizards who built the Castle and the Eee Cee Pee Machine were growing old. We were chosen because we were strong and could work well with the big Machine parts.

"What is an Eee Sea Pea Machine, Mr. Growl-slavver?" asked Earnest Lee, as little Kwi-Kwi peeked out from beneath him.

"Well, there's a poem that I learned on my father's knee. I think it will explain it," said Growl-slavver.

"EVOL was beset by millions of ills
from unbreathable air to toxic waste spills

So the wizards assembled a miracle Machine
it cleaned up the world, made it bright shiny clean

Then the wizards all chanted, 'Just remember one verse'
'Show love for all things, or it could run in reverse!'"

"I still don't understand. What's the Easy-P Machine, Mr Growl-slavver, sir?" asked little Kwi-Kwi, forgetting all about her fright after hearing about the wizards.

"Why don't you come in and see for yourself?" said old Growl-slavver with a smile.

So the two little explorers followed Growl-slavver across the great wooden drawbridge and into the Castle. The noise outside the Castle was like a whisper compared to the tremendous bedlam of racket inside.

All around were gears, sockets, vats, and wheels making groans, bubbles, squeaks, and squeals.

"This is the Eee Cee Pee Machine that we Grundlebork have always taken care of," said Growl-slavver proudly with a sweep of his hand. The great Machine seemed to fill the whole Castle. "I was left in charge of it by my father, and I've done everything he told me to do. Only now it seems to be running backwards, and it's pushing out all kinds of foul vapors and liquids. I can't seem to make it run the way it used to," said Growl-slavver forlornly. As he spoke a single tear trickled down his whiskered cheek.

The two friends were astounded by the huge Machine. They had never seen any kind of Machine before, and they were amazed to see the Eee Cee Pee Machine in action. They excitedly ran from room to room pointing and exclaiming at all the strange turnings and grindings of the huge wheels and levers.

Suddenly, Earnest stopped dead in his tracks. "Look!" he shouted and pointed up to the belly of the largest vat they had seen yet. On the side, he could still make out some words that were almost hidden under centuries of dust and grime. He slowly sounded out the four words, "E-MO-TION COM-MO-TION POL-LU-TION MACHINE!" So this was where Growl-slavver got the initials, E C P!"

"What does EMOTION COMMOTION POLLUTION MACHINE mean, Earnest Lee?" asked Kwi-Kwi. "I've never heard of a Machine before. We did have some stories about the wizards, but nothing about the Machine. Have you ever heard of the EMOTION COMMOTION POLLUTION MACHINE before, Earnest Lee? What do you think it means? Do you know Earnest Lee? Do you?"

"I'm trying to figure it out!" said Earnest Lee sharply. All of Kwi-Kwi's talking combined with all the noise from the great Machine was starting to make Earnest Lee upset.

He was also getting angry at himself for not being able to figure out what "EMOTION COMMOTION POLLUTION MACHINE" meant. As he became angrier and angrier, he noticed that the Machine was getting louder and louder. He also observed that angry dark smoke was now boiling outside. It almost seemed to mirror his own anger. In a flash, he knew the answer!

He quickly reached down and began tickling Kwi-Kwi under her soft furry neck. Kwi-Kwi was soon giggling with glee and trying to tickle Earnest Lee in return.

Now, Pea-Pops are extremely ticklish, and soon the two friends were both laughing and rolling around on the floor of the Castle. Suddenly, Earnest Lee stopped and put his finger to his lips.

"Shhhhhhhhhh," he said.

Then they listened. Sure enough, much of the earlier clamor made by the EMOTION COMMOTION POLLUTION MACHINE had quieted. Many of the parts were merely clicking instead of hammering, purring instead of clattering.

"Go look outside!" he beckoned to Kwi-Kwi.

"Hey!" exclaimed Kwi-Kwi. "There isn't as much smoke coming out of the Castle now! What's going on, Earnest Lee?"

Earnest Lee just laughed and jumped for joy! "Come on, Kwi-Kwi, we've got lots of work to do!"

"I still don't understand, Earnest Lee," said Kwi-Kwi. "Are we going on another adventure?"

"Just be patient!" said Earnest Lee. "I'll explain on the way. "Earnest Lee told a startled Growl-slavver that they might be able to solve his problem with the Machine. Then the two friends said a quick farewell, raced out of the Castle and scampered down the mountain.

As they were again crossing Skunky-stink Swamp on their raft, Earnest Lee explained to his friend, "Don't you see, Kwi-Kwi? The EMOTION COMMOTION POLLUTION MACHINE takes the emotions of all the people who live on this planet, chews them up and spits them back out. When the people are feeling angry and fighting, their negative emotions get spit back out at them as pollution."

"Then why are you so happy, Earnest Lee?" wondered Kwi-Kwi.

"Just keep on paddling, Kwi-Kwi!" laughed Earnest Lee.

The two friends quickly reached the banks of the Forbidden Forest. Earnest Lee was in such a good mood that he was laughing and giggling all the way back to his village, with Kwi-Kwi running close behind. Soon the two friends had reached the outskirts of Grungemudden.

"Hey, everybody! Ugly Earnest is back!" yelled Drakus as soon as he spied his brother. "And he's got a weird little monster with him!"

The villagers poured from their huts to see what all the commotion was about. When they saw that it was Earnest Lee and some other creature, they crowded around and began yelling and shaking their fists. Most of the villagers were upset because they had lost a good night's shut-eye searching for the missing Earnest Lee. Now that he had returned and was apparently unharmed, their worry turned to anger.

"Wait everyone!" shouted Earnest Lee. "I know how to stop all the pollution! Kwi-Kwi and I discovered an EMOTION COMMOTION POLLUTION MACHINE in the Dark Castle. It's takes all the hateful, angry, crabby and just plain ugly feelings of EVOL and turns them into pollution. We need to love our world, not hate it. We need to help our friends and not fight with them. And most of all, we just need to be happy!"

At the mere mention of the Dark Castle, the crowd became even angrier. No one from their village had ever braved the Forbidden Forest, much less crossed Skunky-stink Swamp. How could a small ugly child like Earnest Lee have even gotten close to the Dark Castle?

"You're making those stories up!" shouted one of the villagers.

"YEAH! LET'S GET HIM!" shouted the rest of the crowd as they shook their fists at Earnest Lee and Kwi-Kwi.

Earnest Lee looked up at the multitudes of poisonous dark clouds that were now boiling out of the Dark Castle.

"Look what you are doing!" he yelled as he pointed toward the billowing smoke. "It's your anger that's making that pollution!"

"It's always making pollution!" the crowd roared back. Earnest Lee realized that talk alone was never going to work. The villagers were much too angry to ever listen to him. He quickly huddled with Kwi-Kwi and whispered something in her ear.

In a rush, the two friends broke apart and began running through the crowd tickling adults and children alike under their sensitive arms. Now, everyone knows that Pea-Pops are very ticklish, and Kwi-Kwi turned out to be the all-time greatest Pea-Pop tickler ever. She was so quick that she could run rings around the bigger and clumsier Pea-Pops. She also was able to tickle not only with her two clever little hands, but with her fuzzy tail as well.

In no time at all, she and Earnest Lee had all the Pea-Pops of the village down on the ground rolling and laughing. Soon the child-pops were tickling the adult-pops, the wife-pops were tickling their husband-pops, and the Grand-pops were tickling their grandchildren-pops. The whole village became one merry mass of bodies and laughter.

Suddenly, there was a flash of lightning and a crack of thunder. "ACID RAIN!" the Pea-Pops all yelled. But it was too late, because at that very instant, it began pouring down huge sheets of rain.

The Pea-Pops' emotions had instantly turned from happiness to fright. But then they noticed that they weren't getting burned! In fact, there was something very different about this rain. It was washing all the grime off the Pea-Pops' faces! It was washing all the dirt off the buildings of Grungemudden. Softly muted colors were appearing where before there had been only grays and browns.

"Look!" shouted several of the Pea-Pops as they pointed towards the ground.

All around, blades of grass and plant leaves were poking out of the spaces between all the trash. In no time at all flowers were blooming in these uncluttered spaces. Soon there was a riot of color such had never been seen before.

"Quick, every Pop!" yelled Earnest Lee. "Let's pick up all the trash so more flowers can grow!"

"What do we do with the trash when we pick it up?" asked several of the Pea-Pops.

"We can store it in the old warehouse. It's been abandoned for years. We can sort it, clean it and reuse it. We can call it our recycling center," said Earnest Lee.

As soon as the flowers started to bloom, little Kwi-Kwi became more fidgety than normal.

"I really need to go back to the Forest, Earnest Lee," she said.

Before Earnest Lee even had a chance to blink, Kwi-Kwi had picked a huge bouquet of flowers and dashed off.

The Pea-Pops, all working cheerily together, soon had their whole village cleared of trash, and, sure enough, even more plants and flowers were springing from the cleared ground. The Pea-Pops were speechless. But this was only the beginning! The rain clouds parted slightly and a tremendously bright light flashed across the sky.

"What-the-POP!" came the chorused yell from all the Pea-Pops as the sun shown through in all its glory. Young and old alike just stood amazed and gaping at the beautiful blinding ball of light that was their SUN!

Earnest Lee was dazzled by all that was happening, and tears of happiness and joy (not to mention the bright sun) came pouring from his eye. He turned, and saw another wonderful thing happen. A great ring of colors formed in the sky, making a perfect rainbow. Then his eye really bugged out!

"Hey everybody, look behind you!" he yelled at the rest of the crowd who were still dazzled by the sun.

"OOOOOOOOOOOOOOOOOOOOO!" was all the Pea-Pops could say. For there, framed by the marvelous and colorful rainbow was a Crystal Castle where the Dark Castle once had stood. It was glinting in the sun and glimmering with all the colors of the rainbow. It was a marvel of marvels on a day of miracles.

When Earnest Lee peered very hard at the Castle, he could barely see the great lumbering shape of Growl-slavver dancing and waving to the Pea-Pops from the top of one of the Castle towers. He even could hear hints of Growl-slavver's thunderous laughter rolling down the mountainside.

The more the Pea-Pops laughed, the more beautiful their world became. That night they had a huge celebration. It was the first celebration that even the oldest of Pea-Pops could remember. They ate and laughed, frolicked and danced. They skipped and tickled, chuckled and pranced. They even shared in the fun with their new-found, furry friends, the Manderill.

Kwi-Kwi had scampered back to the tunnels under the Forbidden Forest (which is now known as the Friendly Forest) to tell of the great transformation that had come over the world.

The legends had come true! The flowers were Kwi-Kwi's proof that the outside world was again safe for the Manderill. That was why she had been anxious to leave earlier.

Kwi-Kwi became an instant hero of the Manderill. Some of the best storytellers even started working on an epic story about her exploits. Soon all the little Manderill could thrill at her adventures, just as she used to be excited by the old legends.

The Manderill and Pea-Pops decided to change the name of their planet from EVOL to EVOL-ution because it had evolved into a beautiful place to live. They also proclaimed little Earnest Lee as EVOL-ution's Official Ambassador of Love, and Kwi-Kwi as the Official Ambassador of Happiness. Everyone laughed and cheered at the proclamation!

Late that night, as the party was starting to wind down, Earnest Lee and Kwi-Kwi slipped outside for a quiet walk. They both received their last surprise for the day! The entire night sky was covered with about a jillion sparkling dots of light!

"Those are stars, Earnest Lee!" squeaked Kwi-Kwi in amazement. "It's just like our fables said! They are all supposed to be glowing balls just like our sun, only they are so far away that they look like dots."

Earnest Lee looked up into the glories of the heavens. It seemed like he could see forever. "I wonder if there are other planets circling around those stars that just might need my love too?" he asked with a wink and a smile and a tickle under Kwi-Kwi's chin.

The End

About the author:

Alan Warble is a 42 year old professional photographer turned computer programmer with Purdue University. A graduate of Indiana University, he resides in West Lafayette, Indiana. He enjoys the companionship of his wife, Lynn, his daughter, Michelle, and their Weimeraner dog, Joya.

Alan is a part-time inventor who recently patented the "I Love You, Earnest Lee" doll. The doll is based on the book's character, who says "I Love You" every time you look at it.

For leisure, Alan is active with a local group which recreates life of the 17th century French-Canadian Voyagers. He has a great love for children, photography, nature and fishing. (And he is yet to catch the elusive three-eyed fish!)

About the illustrator:

Manette M. Wiederhold is a freelance illustrator and graphic designer. She graduated from Ball State University in 1991 and now lives in Lafayette, Indiana with her husband, Marvin, Buster the dog, and Boonie the cat.

Originally from Michigan City, Indiana, Manette always knew she would be an artist. She began drawing at the age of five, and has been inspired by the many styles of Disney. Manette has also been a life-long fan of Charles M. Schultz of "Peanuts" fame.

When Manette is not busy drawing, she plays piano, and enjoys softball or camping with Marvin and Buster.

EARNEST LEE

KWI-KWI (KWEE-KWEE)

SKUNKY-STINK SWAMP FISH

NIGHT-WORM

THE CASTLE

A MANDERILL

A PEA-POP

GROWL-SLAVVER